# This book belongs to:

..........................

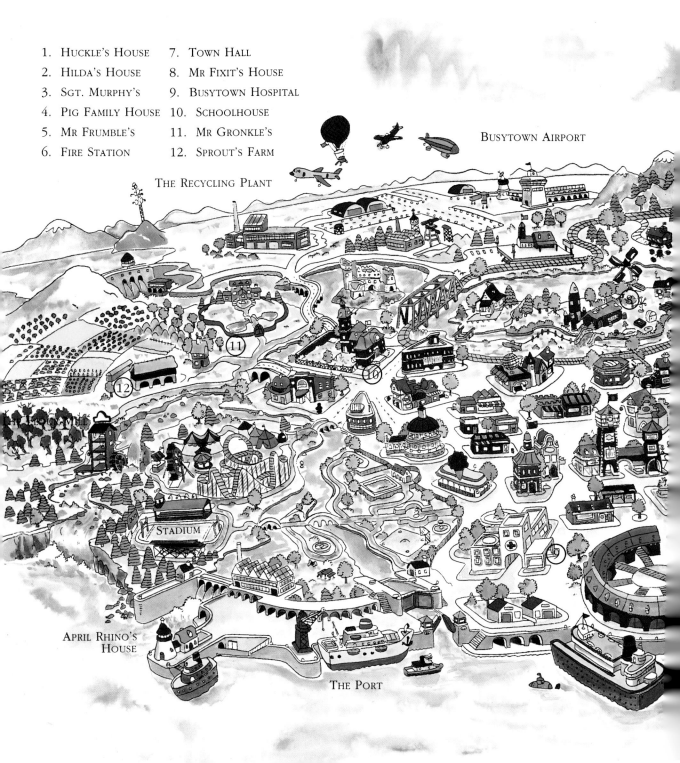

1. HUCKLE'S HOUSE
2. HILDA'S HOUSE
3. SGT. MURPHY'S
4. PIG FAMILY HOUSE
5. MR FRUMBLE'S
6. FIRE STATION
7. TOWN HALL
8. MR FIXIT'S HOUSE
9. BUSYTOWN HOSPITAL
10. SCHOOLHOUSE
11. MR GRONKLE'S
12. SPROUT'S FARM

BUSYTOWN AIRPORT

THE RECYCLING PLANT

STADIUM

APRIL RHINO'S
HOUSE

THE PORT

First published in Great Britain in 1995
by HarperCollins Publishers Ltd,
77-85 Fulham Palace Road,
Hammersmith, London W6 8JB
1 3 5 7 9 10 8 6 4 2
ISBN: 0 00 664573 9
Printed and bound in Italy
Designed and produced by Les Livres du Dragon d'Or

# The Busy World of Richard Scarry

# Busytown Regatta

Collins

*An Imprint of HarperCollinsPublishers*

**DRING! DRING!**
The alarm clock rings
on the bedside table.

"Good morning hat!"
says Mr Frumble,
sitting up.

"Oh, I've just remembered.
It's the Busytown Regatta today.
How I love a boat race!"
Mr Frumble dances around
the room.

**Crassshh!**
Be careful, Mr Frumble!

"Good morning boat!"
says Mr Frumble as he
walks over to the garage.

"Hmmm. Fine wind today. I better hurry, I don't
want to miss the race."
Mr Frumble hops in his pickle car and drives
off with his pickle boat in tow.

But the pickle boat's mast
catches on his neighbour's
clothesline!
**Ping!**
Watch out, Mr Frumble!

Mr Frumble steers his pickle
car through Busytown with the
clothesline flapping from the
mast of his pickle boat.
Oh no! Look out, Mr Frumble!

**Ooooops!**
Mr Frumble just misses
Soybean Goat's fruit truck.

Everyone is getting ready for the Regatta. Sprout Goat puts the finishing touches to his corncob boat,

Bananas Gorilla gives his banana boat a final check and Millie Mouse hoists the sail on her hammer boat.

Huckle and Lowly's boat stands
in the Cat family's drive.

"Wow, Dad! I bet we have the
prettiest boat in Busytown!"
exclaims Huckle.
"I hope it floats," mutters Lowly.
"Don't worry, Lowly," replies Father Cat.
"Now that she's painted, she'll float like
a cork."

Here come Bruno Bear and Miss Honey,
towing a hot-dog boat.
"Good luck for the race!" Sergeant Murphy
shouts out as they pass by.

Mr Fixit raises the sail of his bathtub boat. "Voilà!" he exclaims.

But his boat is too wide and too tall to squeeze through the door!

"Good morning, Mr Fixit," says Hilda as she passes with her hippo dinghy.

Father Cat pushes Huckle and
Lowly's boat off the trailer and
into the water.
"Anchors away!" calls out Huckle.
"Aye, aye, Captain!" Lowly replies.

At last Mr Frumble arrives at the launch ramp.
"Prepare to launch!" he cries.
"Would you like a hand?" asks Father Cat.
"Oh, no thank you. I'm a born sailor," Mr Frumble replies with confidence.

**CLANK!**

**RUMBLE!**

**SPLASH!**

"Shiver me timbers!" says Mr Frumble as he watches his pickle car follow his pickle boat into the water.

At last all the boats are ready for the big race.

April Rhino's Coast Guard
cutter makes its way to the
starting line.
"All skippers prepare for
the Busytown Regatta,"
April calls through the
megaphone.
"Starting time, now!"
**BANG!** goes the starting
cannon.

"They're off!" calls out Father Cat, looking through his binoculars.

Mr Frumble's pickle boat wobbles into sight.

The pickle boat rocks violently from side to side. It zig zags and circles and suddenly veers off towards Bananas' banana boat.
"Watch where you're going, Mr Frumble!" Bananas Gorilla calls out.
But it's too late! **BOOM!**
Bananas Gorilla dives in the water as his boat capsizes.

"Uh oh, here comes Mr Frumble!" shouts Lowly.

The pickle boat is heading straight for them but they manage to get out of the way just in time, thanks to Lowly!

Watch out, Mr Frumble!
**CRASH!**
Mr Frumble's pickle boat cuts Millie Mouse's hammer boat in half!

Fortunately April Rhino is not far behind and she fishes poor Millie out of the water.

Millie watches the rest of the race from the Coast Guard cutter.

**BANG!** Mr Frumble's boat sinks the corncob boat, **BAM!** the hot-dog boat, and **WHAM!** Hilda's hippo dinghy. April Rhino is there to pick up the victims, one after the other.
Mr Frumble races back and forth across Busytown Harbour. He's out of control!

"Mr Frumble must have learned how to sail on a destroyer!" remarks Lowly.

**CLANG!**

Mr Frumble finally crashes into April Rhino's sturdy Coast Guard cutter.

The pickle boat sinks out of sight.
"Oh dear, oh dear, oh dear!" sighs Mr Frumble
as he waits to be rescued.
The few boats that are still afloat approach the
finishing line. Lowly and Huckle zoom across,
just ahead of the others.

"We've won! We've won!"
shout Lowly and Huckle,
jumping up and down.

"I'm so proud of you two sailors!" Father Cat says to Huckle and Lowly. "Thanks Dad," Huckle replies, "but I don't think we can take all the credit – we had a little help from Mr Frumble!"

Here comes April's Coast Guard cutter.
Be careful, Mr Frumble!

**SPLASH!**

Poor Mr Frumble!

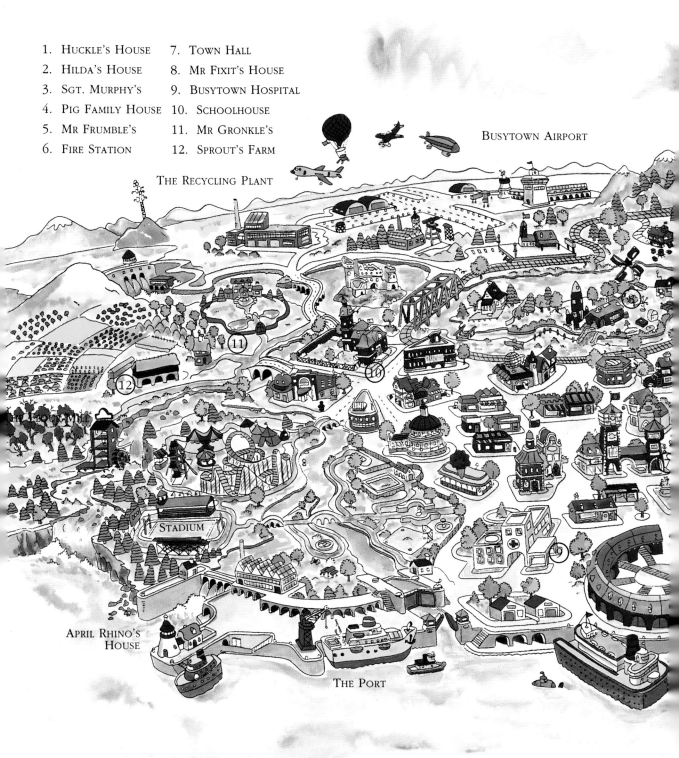

1. HUCKLE'S HOUSE
2. HILDA'S HOUSE
3. SGT. MURPHY'S
4. PIG FAMILY HOUSE
5. MR FRUMBLE'S
6. FIRE STATION
7. TOWN HALL
8. MR FIXIT'S HOUSE
9. BUSYTOWN HOSPITAL
10. SCHOOLHOUSE
11. MR GRONKLE'S
12. SPROUT'S FARM

THE RECYCLING PLANT

BUSYTOWN AIRPORT

STADIUM

APRIL RHINO'S HOUSE

THE PORT